For Whom the Struesel Tolls

For Whom the Struesel Tolls

Forrest Cheatwood

CONTENTS

For Jaymin Ewens: the best sister a moron
like myself could hope for.

Special thanks to Chantel Reeder and
Morgan Wheeler for being willing to put up
with my inane ramblings.

Therefore, send not to know for whom the streusel tolls...

Coffins and Doughnuts

There's no one thing that's true. It's all true.

ERNEST HEMINGWAY

Two hours, thirty-four minutes, fifty-six seconds.
Fifty-seven.
Wait.
No, it goes down, you idiot. It's a countdown.
Fifty-five.
Wait, how many seconds passed?
Son of a...

No one told Germaine how dull it could be working at a coffin store. Even with the added responsibilities of a barista, there was rarely anything to do. His boss, Mr. Ilkmeyer, took care of any actual business. Germaine was mostly responsible for helping customers decide which muffin to buy while they perused caskets and urns.

Of course, to do that, there had to be customers. Oddly enough, the store wasn't a hive of activity most days. It was almost as if people weren't dropping dead like mayflies every twenty-four hours. Nothing more depressing.

Well, perhaps the location was more depressing. Either because Mr. Ilkmeyer was ignorant or a conniving evil genius, the store was positioned next to the local nursing home. Germaine never managed to get an answer from his boss to either effect. He wasn't sure that it mattered, though. He wasn't particularly concerned with any ethical dilemmas at that point in his life. So long as the paychecks kept coming his way, he'd work. Selling decaffeinated coffees to seniors he'd eventually be selling urns for somehow didn't bother him. That was probably a bad sign.

Best not to dwell on that, not when he only had two and a half hours left to his shift. This was the endgame. Maybe he'd get lucky and no one would be dead, literally or figuratively, for the next two hours. Wouldn't that be just grand?

Two hours and thirty-two minutes.

Germaine sighed, looking around the store idly. The coffee machine was humming behind him, adding a pleasant ambience of white noise. He would turn on the radio, but he had already heard the same twenty-seven songs yesterday. Why perpetuate the cycle? The simple droning had a better rhythm than most of those songs anyways.

He picked up one of the muffins that had survived the day's onslaught of geriatrics. Crumbs rolled out of the thin paper and onto the linoleum as he held it up between his fingers. He studied it, taking note of its misshapen top. It reminded him of a tumor he had seen protruding from a corpse's forehead. The corpse likely had a name at one point, but Germaine quickly learned there was no point in trying to remember all of the names of the stiffs that ran through his little corner of the world. He always forgot them in an hour.

He put the muffin back with the other atrocities and stretched his arms out. Something popped in one of his shoulders, but he didn't know which. He shook his arms out and let them fall back to his sides. His fingers started to tap alongside the coffee machine's percussion.

Germaine surveyed the selection of urns that were on display. The range was quite impressive, really. There was the standard fare of metallic and bronzed urns, each with the option of custom inlays for names and designs. Boring choices, but affordable and, at least, elegant in some sense. Fancier options for the prestigious, such as Grecian urns and urns designed after those Chinese vases (what was it, Ming?), existed in their own section. Might as well be separated in death as in life, after all. And then there was the section that Germaine dubbed "The Aisle of Misfit Urns." It wasn't a particularly clever name, he thought, but he had yet to think of anything better. Regardless, it was apt. The aisle in question consisted of oddities, knick-knacks, that family members could retire their "loved" ones to for all of eternity. Some looked to be just like any other urn, but featured some sort of tacky cartoon or phrase. His current favorite was one that had an image of the Mother Mary with the phrase "Bless you, child. You're going to need it." He wasn't sure, but, given its slightly smaller size, he assumed it was a tactless design for a child born to judgmental parents. Some of the misfits weren't content with being a standardized shape, though. That's where it got truly interesting. There were urns shaped like cars, airplanes, and boats, fish, eagles, and dogs, houses, banks, and doctor's offices. There was even one that was just a disembodied head. It didn't appear to be of anyone famous or important. It was just some guy with a hollow smile and lecherous eyes. The dead probably shouldn't be allowed to leer after the living as far as Germaine could figure. Next to the head were two urns that Germaine was convinced were related: a urinal and a fire hydrant. He just wasn't sure if the urinal was for a person and the fire hydrant for a dog or if it was reversed. Still, nothing quite compared to the one that was a sculpture of a coffin with a tiny elder dancing upon the lid. Underneath it was written, "And you thought you cheated me out of a dance."

The coffins were a bit tamer. There weren't any outlandish shapes or disembodied heads. Maybe that was only due to the fact that they had to fit grave plots. Otherwise, Germaine was sure, there would be a coffin shaped like a giant head, complete with a devilish grin. Instead, the creepiest design amongst the coffins was what Germaine had labeled "The Lenin Special." It was a typical coffin, but with a glass lid. He didn't see the point since the lid would only be useful during a visitation as a sneeze guard. After that, the glass was only going to be covered by dirt. Perhaps it was for the worms, so they at least knew that there was a prize in the box.

Germaine crossed his arms on the top of the glass that guarded the pastries and rested his head in their crux. It was spring, so the Sun was starting to take on the habits of a teenager. It was just as well. The extra light aided in the insertion of keys into cars at the end of the day. The same thought process could probably be applied to the Armageddon. All those fiery meteorites and lava-spewing crevasses would likely provide all sorts of visibility.

As he pondered the inevitable demise of civilization and its meager luxuries, the monotonous clanging that signaled the entry of some interlopers. Germaine turned his head slowly, his eyes squinting into the yellowed light. It was a couple. At least as far as Germaine was concerned, it was a couple. They came through the door chatting each other up, their arms were around each other, and their faces were close. He squinted harder despite the light being out of his eyes.

The two, a man and a woman, ignored Germaine immediately. That didn't bother him. It made his life easier when the customers ignored him. It was only common courtesy to do the same.

Shifting his attention back to the buzzing of the coffee, Germaine pulled himself from the glass, his arms leaving blurry streaks. He looked down at his feet and scuffed the floor. The cheap linoleum was marred by all manner of dark streaks and blotchy scars. He let himself smile and nod his head for a moment. The floor of petty victories.

"Do you think that one is big enough?"

Germaine heard a strange voice echo through the store. He gradually straightened himself up, his eyes wide and curious. It wasn't a crotchety voice coming from a crotchetier retiree ordering a bran muffin with a prune shoved on top (Germaine called them enemuffins). No, it was a young one coming from a younger person. He knew it had to be the woman that had just walked in, but he was still confused. Perhaps it was the question she posed.

"I don't know," the guy responded. "It might be too big."

They were standing by the coffins. They were obscured by shelves of ash-holders, but it wasn't hard to notice when something was moving in a funeral parlor. Particularly if it wasn't located in the kitchen area. Germaine was just glad that he knew someone else that was living was in the store.

"Approximately how big do you think he was?"

"You saw him as well as I did. He's not that large. Maybe five feet."

"Are you counting the uh…"

"Of course I am. How could I not be?"

Funeral arrangements. Not that big of a deal. Germaine was a tiny bit perplexed as to why they were whispering. There was no one else in the store, aside from himself and that roach he found living in a muffin underneath the stove, so it couldn't be a courtesy issue. Maybe they were just quiet people. Germaine was always told that he was a quiet sort of person, but he figured that was due more to his refusal to speak to other humans. Still, it was plausible.

"Do you think we should get a smaller box, then?" the woman asked. "A separate one, I mean."

"What? Like an actual head case?"

The coffee machine's dull buzzing abruptly died. Germaine arched his back and stretched his arms in an exaggerated manner. The couple didn't seem to notice that the ambience of the parlor had taken a slight turn. Germaine knew the risk of shutting the machine off. Nothing would be there to hardly mask the noises of a grown man sneaking about a store for the recently, or soon-to-be, dead. At the same time, though, nothing would be there to hardly mask the noises of a grown couple discussing how they decapitated a guy.

The benefits outweighed the cons, he figured.

"Is that a thing people do?"

"Probably not normal people, no."

Germaine, seizing the dry mop that was resting against the refrigerator, started to pantomime doing his job. The mop's brushes hovered just above the floor, taunting the dust and crumbs like an axe-headed pendulum. He had realized that actually performing the activity of sweeping would have generated more audible sound than the machine. He couldn't gamble too much, after all.

"He wasn't terribly normal, though, was he?" The woman was sizing up a few of the coffins, tilting her head at a ponderous angle.

The man, holding his hands apart as though he were holding a basketball, was crouched next to an oak box that was meant for children. As he pulled himself back up, he said, "I guess not, but I'm not sure how you would bury that mess."

"Would they need a second plot?"

"Crap. You don't think they would, do you?"

"What a surprise, I don't have an answer to a question I posed."

Germaine sidled up to one of the shelves and leaned conspicuously against it like an awkward sweep-carrying bookend. He cautiously stuck his nose out from behind the wooden support and realized that he couldn't see through his nostrils, so he willed himself to poke his head out far enough that his eyes could bear witness.

"Fair enough. Although, I'm not so sure that they would require a second plot. They could probably just fit the head box into the space it would have occupied anyways, you know?"

"I think I'm more worried about explaining why we had to buy a separate case for a man's disembodied face."

"I wouldn't worry about that. It's all a business, right? The more we spend, the less they care. We'd probably only be questioned if we decided to staple the head back on."

There was a slight ruckus as a few urns bobbled into each other. Germaine had overestimated the sturdiness of his resting position and had slipped forward, bumping the shelf just enough off-balance that it caused the stir in the ceramics. The couple looked up in time to see a discarded dry mop coming to rest between the rows of urns.

Undeterred, the man returned to his perusing of depressive wares. The woman, curious as to why a dry mop would materialize to disturb future graves, looked around the aisles. When she failed to notice the slightly less dead grin next to the lifeless smile of a poorly conceived design, she rejoined the search for the perfect pine box.

"I doubt that, but it's a thought."

"Oh, now would you look at that. Seriously, do you see this?"

"If you are referring to Cinderella's final slipper, then yes."

"It might have been easier to go with the Sleeping Beauty reference, you know."

"Which one is more fun to say, though?"

"I see your point."

Germaine, every word he could remember from his time in junior high gym class running through his mind, stared at the cleaning implement that had threatened his operation. He carefully removed his head from the shelf and slunk down to the floor. Not wanting to touch the ground with his bare hands, he resorted to an uncomfortable method of crouch walking. He made his way back around the stiff rack and, without pausing in his cartoonish gait, grabbed the mop and disappeared behind another wall of mortuary goods.

"I can't believe this sort of thing even exists," the woman muttered. "It seems so... tacky."

"You know someone is interested in that. There's always someone who wants that creepy fairytale ending."

This was true, Germaine had learned. The store had only managed to sell one of the cases, but it happened within the first month of their arrival. Mr. Ilkmeyer had only purchased two when he placed the order, fearing that they wouldn't be popular, but one Ms. Jacobs had met an unfortunate end at a young age shortly after they arrived. Her father, thinking that it was, actually, the same sort of case Lenin was resigned to, bought the coffin without a second thought. He didn't want his daughter's youth to fade. Not many did. However, most also recognized that magical crystal coffins didn't exist and Lenin's beauty sleep was the product of embalming. Mr. Ilkmeyer once proposed the option of embalming, but, when slapped with a lawsuit from the government, quickly learned that taxidermy was not the same process.

"I guess it might startle potential grave robbers," the woman mused.

"I don't think we need one, though. It would ruin the closed casket look in our case."

"Not if you carefully positioned the head so it was aligned properly."

"Right, but unless we did sow it back on, one jostle is all it takes to give him the Antoinette treatment."

"Might liven up the moment."

"Might result in repeat business for the parlor, more like."

They kept bringing up funeral arrangements, Germaine finally noticed. Headless corpse or not, suspicion of Bonny and Clyde being criminals started to fade in his mind and they started to sound more like Phoebe and Joey. He shook his head. He needed to stop reading fanfics in his spare time.

Tossing the sweep lightly upwards, Germaine caught the handle with a quick inward swing of his arm and shuffled back to behind the counter. He lazily looked at the clock. *Two hours and twelve minutes.* Time never flew for Germaine, even if he strapped it into an airplane traveling across international time zones.

There was a lull in the conversation all of a sudden. The room fell deathly silent. It made him uncomfortable. He considered reviving the coffee machine from its slumber, but he knew it would just have to be killed later. Instead, he turned to the decrepit radio that permanently rested next to the cash register. He stared at the knobs and buttons for a moment, imagining a robotic face was staring right back. He grabbed one of its eyes and twisted until something clicked. A strangled voice started to emanate from the multi-holed mouth and Germaine thought he had tuned into an attempted murder. But no, it was nothing so interesting. It was just a DJ introducing some song from the fifties whose performer was more than likely in the ground somewhere. Or performers, to be fair. Not that he cared. He twisted the eye back into its original position.

"Did you hear music for a second there?" the man whispered.

"Yes. Now, have you given any thought to cremation?"

"I have, but I'm still not sure it's the best idea."

"But why? It removes the need for a coffin."

"What about the head, though? Would we still get that a box?"

"Wait... what are you talking about? Are you talking about a partial cremation?"

"Well, sure. Isn't that what you were suggesting?"

"No. Absolutely not. Why would we only incinerate one half of a person?"

"'One half?' So now a head is half of a person?"

"You know what I mean."

"Okay, fine, but I do have to ask then: If we cremate can we just fill that cistern in the backyard with dry wood, soak him in kerosene, and toss him down there with a few matches? I mean, it would be cost-effective."

Oh dear Lord, Germaine perked up, *they* are *murderers*. Headlines spun in his brain and he thought for sure that he heard sirens blaring from outside. The cops would surround the parlor and yell at the couple through dirty white cones. A shoot-out would erupt, he knew, and one of them would be shot dead while the other finally surrenders to the police. The worst part of it all, though, would be that Germaine would have to appear in court as a witness. He'd have to sit through hours and hours of proceedings and listen to jargon spouted off by overpaid "officials." The survivor of the pair might even swear some form of vendetta against him and he'd have to enter Witness Protection and become some sort of lumberjack in the wilds of Montana, roughin' it and fending off ravenous beavers every day and night from his livelihood.

Didn't sound half bad when he actually considered it.

"Cost-effective, yes, but how would that affect property value?" the woman asked.

"Who would know?"

"Aside from us? I don't know, but we do have some fairly nosy neighbors. That Mr. Ackenridge is always watching us."

"You mean he's always watching me."

"I'd argue a little of both. The point is, he'd know. I know he would."

Call the cops, call the cops, call the cops... Nah, that would require work, wouldn't it? It wasn't in Germaine's nature to complicate his life. Besides, whoever it was, Germaine probably didn't know him. All he wanted at this point was for the two conspirators to leave, maybe buy a stale coffee, and never return. Wouldn't that be grand?

"Look, we can stand here all day bickering about this *or* we can just make a decision here and now. I don't really want to stand around surrounded by the world's creepiest monuments to human existence."

"Losing our nerve are we?"

"Yeah, alright, I guess I am."

Germaine felt a pressure leave him and the new-found hollowness made him lighter. He stood up straight behind the counter and flattened his shirt hurriedly. His name tag was hanging crooked like a broken sign, but he didn't bother refastening it, hoping that his name was obscured by its position. His lips quivered lightly as he forced them into a limp facsimile of what might be interpreted as a smile.

The couple reemerged from the dust-covered wares and started toward the door. They stopped for a moment as they noticed Germaine standing beside shriveled and crusty delectables. They whispered something to one another, nodding and smiling, before approaching the counter, the man rummaging for his wallet.

"How much for a, uh, I'm assuming that's a doughnut?"

Germaine nodded. He pointed to the price tag, the artificial grin still plastered on his face.

"Right. Could we get two of those and two cups of coffee? Smalls. It's getting late, after all. Wouldn't want to be awake all night, would we?" The man chuckled lightly as he pulled some bills from his money pouch.

Germaine's head continued bobbing as he got out two Styrofoam cups and began filling them with cooled black liquid. Hopefully the couple liked their coffee cold. He placed plastic lids on both and put them down on the counter. Turning to the pastries, he threw a duo of stiff ones into a sack and tossed it next to the coffee. When he looked back up at them, the couple was conversing in hushed tones, but he couldn't make it out. It was probably something about their next victim. *He* could be their next victim. His eyes widened involuntarily, yet he managed to shrink them before the psychopaths noticed.

"So, how much with tax?" the man questioned.

Germaine opened his mouth to answer, but re-considered when he thought of his future. Instead of saying "17.50" as he was about to, he croaked out, "Nothing. Enjoy."

The couple looked at him as though Germaine were offering anthrax pills, but then smiled once more. They thanked him, grabbed their ill-gotten goods, and started out the door. As they reached the door, Germaine noticed the man slipping the woman a few bucks, shaking his head with one of those admiring tones, if head shaking could have tones.

Confused, Germaine shook his own head. Perhaps it was just a dream. Perhaps his mind, in a state of extreme boredom, had concocted the experience. That had to be it. He was daydreaming. No one was headless and no one was burning bodies in cisterns. He sighed, accepting this new faith. Out of habit, he looked up at the clock.

Two hours and ten minutes.

Great. It's broken.

Fantastic.

Road-Crossed Lovers

" There will always be people who say it does
not exist because they cannot have it.
But I tell you it is true and that you have
it and that you are lucky even if you
die tomorrow."

ERNEST HEMINGWAY

Across the tumultuous highway, she noticed the sapphire sheen. His feathery coat was a beautiful sky caressing little blue rocks. A wisp of blue crowned his head and sharp black lines framed his elegant face. He truly was a magnificent specimen.

But when had he appeared in her little neck of the woods? She couldn't recall ever seeing him in the area. It's not as if it mattered, really, as he was there, here and now. The only question she needed an answer for was whether or not he would notice her.

Compared to his magnificent plumage, she was nothing. Her coat was nothing more than a mix of dusty browns and greying whites. Her breast hardly even displayed the dulled orange her father's had. What hope was there that she would ever attract such an intriguing fellow as the one across the way? Would he even see her? After all, she was small and part of the bark. He would have to truly look to see her from such a distance.

But he was looking, she noticed. His head had turned, his dark, piercing eyes, quite visible even from afar, locked onto her own. The world might as well have stopped. Her eyes met his, a fervent hope spinning in her mind that her suspicions were confirmed, that he had seen her.

Then he opened his dark beak and sang a short song. Surely it was for her, she mused, for he was gazing her direction as she was gazing in his. Still, she hesitated. She glanced about the developed land, worrying that there was another lovebird seeking his affection. Her fearful eyes rummaged the lands, ever-seeking, but there was no cerulean paramour, no feathered fancy to vie for his affections. Her heart slowed in relief as she leaned slightly out. She gave a brief refrain to his own piece and waited eagerly for his response.

True enough, he heard her call and he responded with yet another verse. His voice was exotic, she thought, and nothing like the repeated cackle of her own. Despite the roaring of the metal beasts, she heard his response clear as day. The lilting harmony of his graceful song danced its way to her like a crisp breeze, free of the arid odors from below.

She let the song sink into her soul, absorbing its very essence, before singing her chords. She put all of her heart into them, filling them to the brim with emotion, no longer fearing mistaken intentions. He was singing to her and she was singing for him.

The brilliant eyes seemed to flash at her. Her heart fluttered in anticipation. He wasn't responding, but she was sensing something. Something exciting. She watched him intently as he started to shake out his angelic wings. What better way to touch the sky than with the sky itself, she pondered. Was he planning on flying over? It was moving so fast, but she didn't mind. She just wanted to sing alongside him with no intrusive beasts between them.

She let herself continue their song without ever looking away from him. She would guide him to her like the sirens of old. Not even the raging sea of metal and pavement would drown her out.

He leapt from the branch, diving downwards only to pull up towards the sky. His wings were unfurled, gathering the wind for the purpose it was made for. He soared effortlessly, his eyes focused on her own. Nothing could prevent their union now.

Nothing, that is, but a passing semi.

Howard, startled by the sudden blue mass of feathers on his windshield, grunted and turned on the wiper blades. The squeaky blades eventually managed to push the disturbance off and onto the highway, allowing Howard a clear view once more.

As he drove on, he muttered something about stupid birds.

3

Chocolate Streusel Bars

Ingredients:

13/4 cups unsifted flour

11/2 cups confectioners' sugar

1/2 cup unsweetened cocoa

1 cup butter or 1 cup margarine, cold

8 ounces cream cheese, softened

1 (14 oz) can sweetened condensed milk

1 egg

2 teaspoons vanilla extract

1/2 cup walnuts or 1/2 cup pecans, chopped (optional)

Preheat oven to 350 degrees. In a large bowl, combine the flour,
sugar, and cocoa. Cut in the margarine until

crumbly (dry mixture).

Reserving 2 cups crumb mixture, press remaining mixture in bottom

of 13 by 9 inch baking pan.

Bake 15 minutes.

In large mixing bowl, beat cream cheese until fluffy. Gradually

beat in condensed milk until smooth. Add egg and vanilla and mix

well. Pour over prepared crust.

OPTIONAL: Combine nuts with reserved crumb mix.

Sprinkle crumb mix evenly over cheese mixture.

Bake 25 minutes or until bubbly.

Cool and cut into bars. Store covered in refrigerator.

Serve at funerals and visitations for optimal experience.

4

Mortal Wombat

*" Dying was nothing and he had no picture
of it nor fear of it in his mind. "*

ERNEST HEMINGWAY

Carl Marks didn't have much to his name. His house was modest with a cheap futon and a tiny kitchen. His stove was encrusted with red-brown rust and scorch marks from its previous owner who didn't care to elaborate upon how the markings came to be. A similarly marred mini-fridge was huddled in a corner doing its best to preserve a block of cheddar, a bit of ground beef, two bottles of vodka, and two and a half pounds of carrots.

However, Carl had one possession that he prized above all else: his wombat, Joseph. He acquired the small mammal after a pet shop had to close when it was discovered that the owner was in possession of a Siberian tiger, a baby panda, and three polar bear cubs. Joseph, apparently, was not a major concern for the animal control investigators when they raided the place. Carl found the marsupial after the raiding party had left it huddled in its cage munching on diced carrots.

For some reason, Carl found himself ignoring the abandoned chinchillas, boas, and the odd mini stingrays that occupied the same store as he wandered toward a lone cage hidden near the back. The whimpering puppies and crying kittens did not stop his progress, nor did the Shetland pony that was occupying a diminutive pen in the back. Only one animal was getting his attention and that was Joseph.

The bizarre marsupial had the unique appearance of a cross between a hippo and a puppy. Oddly enough, Carl found this abnormal look to be endearing. He stopped in front of the glass cage that kept his future furry friend and simply stared into the dark, beady eyes of Joseph. At that moment, Carl felt a sort of deep-seated connection to the pointy-eared gopher. He knew that the fat wombat would be important to him somehow. Without any further hesitation, Carl picked up the cage, ignoring the strenuous combination of the metal framework and its contents, and carefully carried it back to his hovel.

That was a year ago. Joseph had grown to be the size of a bulldog, but his pudgy demeanor hadn't changed. Carl, however, had lost twenty pounds and his job, but his alcoholism kept itself strong. More important, though, was that Carl's friendship with Joseph had only increased over the past year, or, at least he believed it had. His affection for the wombat gained strength with every passing day.

Nothing would keep them apart.

Yet, on a relatively unoriginal spring day, Carl left Joseph unattended in order to have an interview. Although he didn't enjoy leaving his fuzzy comrade alone for very long, he knew that Joseph would be okay. He had left him by himself several times in order to get groceries and the like, but he never enjoyed it. Nonetheless, Carl knew that some things were necessities. Carrots, for instance, were always needed as a general supplement for both Joseph and himself, to a lesser extent.

However, on that particular day, Joseph was feeling adventurous. In the one year's time that he had lived in Carl's house, Joseph's most adventurous exploit was when he had a spasm that caused him to roll around. Carl just thought that Joseph was being youthful and didn't mind it all. Yet this time, Joseph had a bizarre, almost instinctual urge to escape his little glass quarters. It wasn't natural, after all, for a wombat to be in an aquarium originally intended for a rodent one quarter the size.

Seeing as how Carl was gone for an indefinite amount of time, Joseph saw an opportunity. The chubby animal did its best to lift its bulk up off the bedding of its cage, but its stubbly legs had atrophied and did not want to cooperate immediately. The dog-hippo chittered violently in response as its legs shook under the carrot-enhanced fat of its body. After about ten minutes of hideous convulsions and blood-curdling squealing (the like of which could only be compared to an epileptic pregnant woman in the middle of childbirth under a broken fluorescent), the fat wombat managed to support its own weight on top of its near-broken legs.

With the first victory out of the way, and arguably the toughest, Joseph's mind began to rethink this adventure. Perhaps it would be best if he got his strength back up and rested a few days after a carrot binge. No, even his greedy mind could recognize that such a plan would only result in a lapse. It was now or never. His next task was to scale the orange plastic doghouse that was intended for sleep, though Joseph was never able to fit inside. It was finally time to put the blasted monstrosity to use.

Putting one stump in front of another, Joseph gradually crossed the four inches that had been between him and the house. Once there, he slowly reached up, risking the momentary pressure on his hind legs as he raised his forward paws up to grip the edge of the roof. The stress on his legs forced another grunt of discomfort, but his front paws latched onto the edge sure enough.

Taking a breather, Joseph surveyed his goal. Outside of his glass prison there was a whole world outside. There was the broken chair that his good friend Carl sat upon while conversing with Joseph. There was the busted stove and the rusted fridge where the glorious carrots were kept. Then there was the portal to a separate world. A brighter world. A new world. Joseph had seen strange winged creatures that made bizarre chirps through that square-shaped gate. And there were other noises that emanated from beyond it, as well. Strange, terrifying growls and honks. Noises Joseph couldn't understand, but, for some unexplained reason, he wanted to. He needed to.

His strength restored, Joseph set about the task in front of him. Pushing down onto the roof, Joseph scratched at the base of the house with his hind legs, trying desperately to climb up it. He scrambled with his front paws to pull himself further up it in an attempt to get better footing. He slipped once or twice before he finally managed to scale the roof. Victory number three.

Thankfully, Carl always left the top of the cage open. He had never had any inclination to believe that Joseph would attempt a daring escape. Joseph never had such an inclination until that moment.

Nonetheless, Joseph found a spot on the doghouse that allowed him access to the lid's edge. Employing the same tactic as he had to get on top of the house, the round furball gripped the edge of the lid and attempted to pull himself up. This time, though, he felt an urgent need to climb quickly. It wasn't adrenaline by any means, but it was rather the byproduct of his mass caving the roof in on the hideous orange house. Before he fell into the crumbling mess, Joseph managed to clamber up and out of his home.

He didn't feel too bad about the gaudy construct's destruction, to be honest. Maybe that was another of his victories.

As soon as he was out, Joseph felt his hairs all flow in one direction. Some mysterious hand was petting his entirety. Rather than feel absolute terror at the presence of an invisible being, Joseph instinctually accepted it. It felt familiar, but distant. It was coming from the direction of the portal, Joseph realized, and his urge to reach the intriguing opening grew in intensity. There must be more invisible hands outside.

Working his way carefully into a position from which he could reach the chair, Joseph began to work out the optimal path to the portal. The chair was too far away for him to reach the portal from, but there was a sturdy-looking box right underneath it. If anything would get him to the portal, then it was the box.

Rolling off the chair and onto the floor, Joseph scurried over to the box as quickly as possible. It took him a little under two minutes to scale the side of the box in the same manner that he had climbed out of his cage with. His journey was coming to an end and he was feeling stronger. The box was nothing at this point. The end was just a little further.

He could feel more of the invisible hand as he rested on top of the box. It was warm and soft. It was inviting him up to the portal. Somewhere beyond the portal, Joseph heard the singing of the intriguing creatures. They were like a welcoming choir to him. He would soon join them, he knew.

Carl would be proud.

Employing his climbing skills for a final time, Joseph hoisted his blubber up onto the ledge and into the light of the glorious portal.

And it was glorious.

A bright orb, like the one that hung over Carl's chair, but so much brighter and warmer, shone down upon the land. It was warm like the hands, but Joseph was forced to squint at the newfound light. Nonetheless, he knew it was a magnificent orb, not a malevolent one. It was wonderful.

And the hands... They only came more frequently and felt stronger. Joseph felt at one with the world, though he did not know what that meant. He just knew it was good, as with the orb in the sky.

One of those creatures flew past his face, chirping as it did so, beckoning Joseph to join in. It looked so free. So happy. And it looked incredibly simple.

Joseph looked down. It was quite a drop, but the ground looked inviting. There didn't seem to be any true consequence either way. The lush ground below looked like his cage's bedding: soft and cushy.

At that moment, Joseph knew his adventure was just beginning. Taking the friendly creature's suggestion, he leaped into the sky.

The hands were all over him now, lifting him

up and into the heavens. He would greet that orb and visit the whole world. All it took was a little nudge from a friendly creature and he was...

Carl watched as something plushy fell from the side of his apartment building. The little brat near the top of the building must have thrown one of her toys out the window in a flurry of excitement. The brown fluffy object bounced heavily on the ground with an odd squeak and *whump*. Carl shrugged absently. The interview hadn't gone the best. When the employer learned that Carl was living in a beaten down shack of an apartment with a wombat, he laughed in his face. Something about Carl's miserable situation was amusing to the fat cat.

It didn't help his situation when Carl threw the man's coffee back into his face and then yanked his tie so that his face would smash into his desk.

It just didn't go well.

And now the unruly temperament of the child upstairs was going to disrupt his day further. He let a deep sigh escape his body as he started towards the door to the building. As he neared it, he glanced back to the fallen toy.

He froze in terror.

There, in the brown, untended grass was the body of Joseph. His furry friend had leapt to his death.

It seemed that, despite his strongest wishes, Joseph was, in fact, a mortal wombat.

Life Insurance

> *There is only now, and if now is only two days, then two days is your life and everything in it will be in proportion.*

ERNEST HEMINGWAY

"I'll stop drinking when the street sweeper comes through."

"So are you planning on drinking for five straight hours?"

"I've got nothing better to do."

"You'll die from alcohol poisoning."

"Such is life, eh?"

It was an oddly boring Friday night at McHaggerty's Pub. Geoff, the bartender, was leaning against the liquor shelves, wringing a towel repetitively. The only other person in the pub was Burl, a regular at McHaggerty's. He was resting his elbows on the stained counter, a tumbler of alcohol positioned in front of him. The two of them had been there for three hours and Burl had been drinking since the second minute. He was one of those men who had consumed so much alcohol that his body was partial immune and handled it better than others. It gave him a false sense of security as far as Geoff was concerned.

"Fine, but if you die from all this, I still expect you to settle your bill. Deal?"

"Deal. Take all my money, I don't care. It's not like I have a will, y'know?"

"Any particular reason?" Geoff shifted his weight slightly against the hardwood of the shelves.

"Why bother dealing with lawyers and junk? I mean, I know what I want done with me when I die, but I don't care who gets all my crap. Friggin' junkies can have it all if they want. That would require some form of initiative on their part, though, so I doubt they'll take it all."

Geoff shook his head with a slight grin as he watched Burl chug his drink and slam it back down. Burl gestured with his hand for another and Geoff reluctantly poured beer into the tumbler. He placed it in front of his drunk friend and returned to his leaning.

"The only thing I care about," Burl continued, "is that my body gets liquefied, filtered into ten different beakers, and then each one shot into space. That's all."

"I'm going to forego the 'why' on this one and ask how you intend to pay for it, instead."

"I'll be dead. They have to honor my last wishes, right?"

"No. That's just... No."

"Well, shoot. Guess they can just throw me in a dumpster then, I guess. I don't care. Just see if they can't get someone to sing 'Goodnight Demonslayer' or something. I don't give a crap anymore. They won't just honor a man's last wish and shoot his liquefied corpse into space? What kind of society do we live in?"

"One that recognizes how creepily bizarre certain peoples' last wishes are." Geoff remarked, noticing that the door of the pub was opening. Perhaps the place would start to fill up after all.

"It's not a creepy wish. I mean, I'm not asking to be stuffed, for what it's worth. I know a guy that did that, by the way. His family kept him in a glass display case in their living room."

"Was that the guy that they kept perpetually reading that issue of the *New York Post* with the story about a headless corpse in a topless bar?" Burl looked over his shoulder to see a familiar face approaching the stool next to him.

"What brings you here, Kat?" Geoff asked, getting a glass out of the cupboard. He knew what she would want. It was always a Long Island.

"I thought I would stop by and see how my two favorite men are doing. Was I right, Burl? About the body?"

"Of course you were. You're the only other person I know of who would know that story."

"We were talking about what to do with Burl's corpse after he drinks himself to death," Geoff said, putting the finishing touches to the Long Island. "He's planning on drinking until the sweeper comes through."

"That's quite a time, Burl. To what does the street sweeper owe the honor of being used as a death toll?" Kat took the Long Island, smiling in thanks to Geoff.

"I guess I'm just a bit fed up is all. Nothing terribly special. I just thought I had my life in order and now it's clear that I don't. It's a typical story, I know."

"I didn't know you managed to get your life in order. Congratulations, Burl!" Kat took a long drink, smiling wryly.

"Screw you, Kat." Burl downed his beer and immediately gestured for Geoff to fill it again. "I had it in order for a few years now."

"So what ruined it?"

Burl waited, his fingers tapping in a broken rhythm, his eyes fixed pointedly on his empty glass. Geoff, sighing heavily, took the glass and started to fill it yet again. Seeing that his drink was being handled, Burl turned to face Kat.

"What ruined it? Easy, my dear Kat. I found out that the very field I had worked so hard to get into was nothing more than the very thing I despised. I felt lied to. Cheated. Scammed. Apparently, I am stuck living in a world that is constantly trying to disappoint me. At least something is succeeding in its goals."

"So you plan on drinking yourself to death instead of rectifying anything?"

"Kat, allow me to introduce you to Burl, a regular here at McHaggerty's," Geoff cheerily announced. "I'm surprised you haven't met yet."

"It takes a real bartender to mock his own customers in their presence," Burl coughed. He was swaying slightly, but his center of balance was anchored against the counter's support. "But to answer your question, Kat, yes. Until a better alternative presents itself, I will drink myself into a stupor. It's a jolly old time."

"Does this pub even have that level of alcohol, Geoff?"

"Well, it's not a particularly busy night, as you can see, but if he continues at this pace, then I really can't say."

"Shouldn't you be cutting him off? Can't you get fired for this?"

"He thinks I haven't been paying attention, but he's been steadily replacing all of my alcohol with water, Kat. I would fight him, but what's the point?" Burl smiled weakly before finishing another drink.

"Kind of defeats your plan, doesn't it? You won't be drinking yourself to death, after all."

"That would be implying that I cared about whatever plan I had to begin with. Plans get ruined too easily for me to bother with them. At this point, it's more of a principle than anything else. Besides, I can still drink myself to death. It will just be more akin to drowning as opposed to poisoning."

"Good to know you have that figured out, I suppose."

"So you don't think plans solve anything, huh?" Geoff got a clean mug from the dusty shelves and started to fill it with some cola. He pulled a screeching stool across the floor to behind the bar and sat down, facing Burl and Kat.

"They inevitably breakdown. No plan is foolproof." Burl lifted himself upright in his seat. His eyes squinted, clearly trying to focus the world around him. "It's a simple matter of Murphy's Law."

"Have you ever considered creating a life plan?"

"What are you? A friggin' high school guidance counselor? I don't need this."

"It's not a bad idea, Burl," Kat chimed in, burping slightly. "It could give you some perspective. Couldn't hurt."

"What if it does hurt? What if I make this plan and then some tiny, insignificant thing throws it completely off track? What if I get my hopes up only to have them be dashed against the concrete like a child's G.I. Joe?"

"Why a G.I. Joe?" Geoff asked.

"I don't know, but I remember seeing some kid throwing theirs forcibly at the sidewalk one afternoon. They don't quite ragdoll like a real person would, but their hips tended to separate. I imagine that was because the rubber band inside would either snap or fall off. It felt fitting."

"I don't know why that felt fitting to you, but okay," Kat half-whispered, taking a longer drink from her Long Island. Geoff, watching her do so, started to wonder if she had eaten anything prior to arriving.

"It just did, okay. I can't explain it."

The door opened behind them and Geoff immediately recognized the smiling face that came bounding through the door. The smiling face was accompanied by several thick binders cradled lovingly within its arms.

"Good evening, cherished friends!" the face called out. The warm, fuzzy intent of the greeting caused Burl to curl up against his drink, cringing. He knew the person, as well. It was Ivan, the stereotypical young and hopeful idealist. He was Burl's kryptonite. It was for this reason that Geoff enjoyed Ivan's presence.

"Well, hello, Ivan," Geoff responded, his smile growing slyly. "Are you here for a drink?" Geoff started to get up from his stool, but Ivan shook his head, the smile never leaving his face.

"No, nothing for me, thank you. I just came by to share with you all my new accomplishment!" As he sat down next to Burl, Ivan slammed the binders onto the counter, the noise ringing in the stale air. He ceremoniously flipped open the top binder, the sudden breeze sending a loose napkin flittering across the counter. "I have finally done it!"

He paused, looking at the trio he had barged in

on. He was clearly waiting for a response, but none of them were biting. Undeterred, he continued, "I have plotted out my entire life, day by day, until my one hundred and sixteenth birthday!"

All three turned to look at him, bewilderment prominently displayed.

"Why?"

"Well, I figured that I could save myself a lot of aggravation in the future by creating an in-depth plan of my future. Every day for the next ninety years, I will know what to do with myself and how to act. I don't have to worry any longer!"

"Are we on the set of *Cheers* or *Happy Days* or something?" Burl muttered, settling back against the counter.

"What is he talking about?" Ivan asked.

"Your timing is impeccable, let's just say that," Geoff answered. "I am curious, though, as to how your plan works, exactly. No one can play out every single day of their lives for ninety years and... No, seriously, why exactly one hundred and sixteen?"

"I did some research the other day and found that the oldest recorded man in history lived to be one hundred and sixteen. Now, as long as I follow my plan to the 'T', then I should be able to live that long. Any time after that day, of course, is completely free for me to do what I want. Pretty great, huh?"

"You planned everything, then?" Burl started. He noticed that Ivan was rapidly bouncing a pen in his right hand and, in a moment of absolute immaturity, slapped the pen out of Ivan's fingers and skittering across the cold floor. For a moment, no one said anything, all eyes watching the pen slide under a vacant table. As it came to rest, Burl turned back to look at Ivan and said, "You plan for that?"

Ivan, not missing a beat, took another pen out of his pocket, clicked it, and scribbled something into one of the binders. Clicking the pen once more and returning it to his pocket, he returned, "It's in there now."

"But you didn't plan for it."

"Right, but I allowed time for such a hiccup to occur, effectively planning for it."

"But you didn't plan for that specifically."

"I know that, but every day I mapped out has room for the little unexpected events. I can't plan for every specific occurrence, after all. I'm not omnipotent, Burl."

"But that's what I'm saying, annoying child," Burl wheezed. The alcohol was starting to hit some part of his system. He just couldn't figure out what. "You can't plan out every day. It doesn't work that way."

"It will be hard, I know," Ivan started to idly flip through the pages. "However, I believe that I can manage it. Diligence can get a body far, y'know? With this plan, I can't possibly fail."

Burl finished his umpteenth drink of the night and immediately asked for a refill. Geoff, knowing the look in his friend's eyes, filled it promptly, but didn't water it down. Burl chugged the drink as soon as it was placed before him. Slamming the mug poignantly in front of him, Burl swiveled in his stool towards Ivan, a finger pointing threateningly at the boy. His face contorted as words were forming in the back of his mind, but nothing managed to escape his lips. He kept changing the face as new words formed, but never left. Eventually, he settled back to his drink.

Kat, drink almost gone, decided to join the conversation, saying, "Hey, Ivan? Did you include getting a life in that plan of yours?" She barely finished before she started to giggle uncontrollably. To Geoff's surprise, Burl started to giggle alongside her. The two of them looked as though they were sharing some sort of super-secret joke exclusive to them.

"Don't mind them, Ivan," Geoff said, his arms crossed. "One of them is a bit tipsy and the other is a cynical shell of hopelessness. I think it's great that you have created some goals to aspire to. Congratulations."

"These aren't goals I'm 'aspiring' to," Ivan spat the word. He was dead serious. "These are events that will occur in my life. I'll make sure of it."

Geoff, only now realizing the sincerity in the kid's voice, started to choke on something. He knew what it was, but to Ivan, it sounded like he maybe just choked on his own spit. Geoff wished he could allow himself to giggle uncontrollably like the two grown children still having a moment in front of him.

"That's... uh, gosh... that's great, Ivan. Good for you. You have it all... all figured out."

Ivan smiled.

Geoff smiled back.

"You two having a moment over here? Sorry to ruin it, but some of us still need drinks. Our life plans dictate it." Burl pushed his mug forward, almost causing it to drop off the edge of the counter, but Geoff stopped it.

"You really shouldn't drink so much, Burl. Aren't you afraid of alcohol poisoning?" Ivan showed genuine worry in his eyes as he asked the question.

"Aren't you afraid of living? I, at least, know that I will have lived before I die."

"Hey now, my plan still has plenty of room for fun, if that's what you are implying."

"I am, I am implying that. You will lead a boring life if this plan works to the 'T' as you say. Of course, knowing that you made this plan leads me to believe you would life a boring life even if it didn't work out. You sound like a boring person."

"Burl, I know you are a bitter man, but now you're just getting mean," Geoff warned.

"No, it's okay, Geoff. This was to be expected

coming here. I'm not bothered by it. I figured I would get this response." His smile grew bigger.

"Yeah, Geoff," Kat murmured, her head resting on her arms, "he's just going to write it in with that pen. It's all part of a plan…"

"You didn't eat anything before coming here, did you? Tsk-tsk, Kat. You should know better." Geoff took the glass from her limp hand and placed it out of reach.

"Well, it's been great, you guys, but I have to get home. I have a big day tomorrow," Ivan said, referring back to his calendar. "Looks like I get promoted tomorrow! Drinks on me tomorrow night, how about that? It's already a date."

He stood up, carefully closed his binder and shuffled them in a neat stack.

"Have a nice evening, you fine people. I will see you on the morrow!"

"Right, have a good night, Ivan," Geoff nodded his head slowly, waving his arm.

The young man bid his final farewell and started towards the door. He stepped outside into the cold night air and shivered slightly. Through the dusty window, he could still see the trio sitting at the counter. They didn't know what awaited them in the days to come. Ivan knew what awaited him, though. He was sure of it. He allowed himself to sigh heavily. It was a shame, really.

There was no point in lingering on the thought. He was wasting valuable life here. He carefully avoided a puddle by the curb and stepped out into the street. No one knows why he never heard the street sweeper, though. He didn't have any hearing deficiency, after all. Nonetheless, Ivan stepped off the curb and into a messily sanitary demise.

Inside the bar, Geoff heard a rather odd sound. He found it akin to the sound of a vacuum sucking in a stale Cheerio. He peered through the dust coated window out into the street and saw the street sweeper stopped in front of his pub. He noticed that something was sticking out from under the brush. It looked distinctly like two legs.

"Holy... Ivan?!" Geoff bolted through the door, leaving Kat and Burl at the counter.

Burl, having heard the street sweeper coming for the past thirty seconds, already had some idea of what had happened. Unperturbed, he reached into his pocket and retrieved a check from his wallet. He knew he shouldn't carry blank checks in his wallet, but he did it anyways. He carefully calculated his tab over the past few hours and wrote out a generous estimate, signed the check, and secured it to the counter with a coaster.

He stood up, straightened his clothes and pat Kat on the shoulder. He started for the door, musing, "Street sweeper came earlier than usual."

...it tolls for thee.